KING CALM

MINDFUL GORILLA IN THE CITY

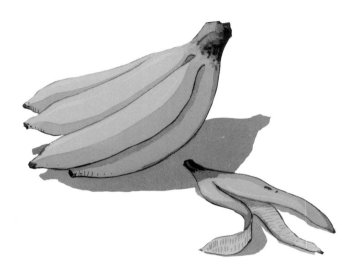

BY **SUSAN D. SWEET**, PHD
AND **BRENDA S. MILES**, PHD

ILLUSTRATED BY
BRYAN LANGDO

MAGINATION PRESS • WASHINGTON, DC • AMERICAN PSYCHOLOGICAL ASSOCIATION

For Grampy and Grandma, who never miss a moment—*SDS*

For Doron, mindful mentor and calming friend—*BSM*

Published by
MAGINATION PRESS ®
An Educational Publishing Foundation Book
American Psychological Association
750 First Street NE
Washington, DC 20002

Magination Press is a registered trademark of the American Psychological Association.

For more information about our books, including a complete catalog, please write to us, call 1-800-374-2721, or visit our website at www.apa.org/pubs/magination.

Book design by Gwen Grafft
Printed by Lake Book Manufacturing Inc., Melrose Park, IL

Library of Congress Cataloging-in-Publication Data

Names: Sweet, Susan D., author. | Miles, Brenda, author. | Langdo, Bryan, illustrator.
Title: King calm : mindful gorilla in the city / by Susan D. Sweet, PhD and
    Brenda S. Miles, PhD ; illustrations by Bryan Langdo.
Description: Washington, DC : Magination Press, [2016] | "American
    Psychological Association." | Summary: Marvin is a calm and mindful
    gorilla living peacefully in the city, enjoying every minute of his day,
    unlike his sassy, curt, irreverent former Empire State-climbing Grandpa.
Identifiers: LCCN 2016005468 | ISBN 9781433822728 (hardcover) |
    ISBN 1433822725 (hardcover)
Subjects: | CYAC: Gorilla—Fiction. | Conduct of life—Fiction. |
    Calmness—Fiction. | Behavior—Fiction.
Classification: LCC PZ7.1.S93 Ki 2017 | DDC [E]—dc23 LC record
available at https://lccn.loc.gov/2016005468

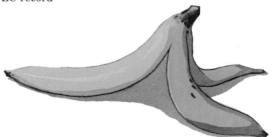

Manufactured in the United States of America
10 9 8 7 6 5 4 3 2 1

In a Great Big City, there lived a gorilla named Marvin.

Marvin wasn't like other gorillas. He didn't
stomp his feet, he never wanted to fight, and he
never ever pounded his chest with a thump thump roar!

He noticed things that many gorillas and people missed.

But Grandpa didn't understand.

"When I was your age, we were wild and ferocious!"
said Grandpa. "Your great grandpa climbed a tall
building, pounded his chest with a thump thump roar,
and everyone called him King! So who are you?"

"I'm Marvin. I'm calm. I'm mindful. That's who I am."

"Well, I guess that makes you King Calm,"
said Grandpa, "whatever that means!"

"I'll show you," said Marvin.

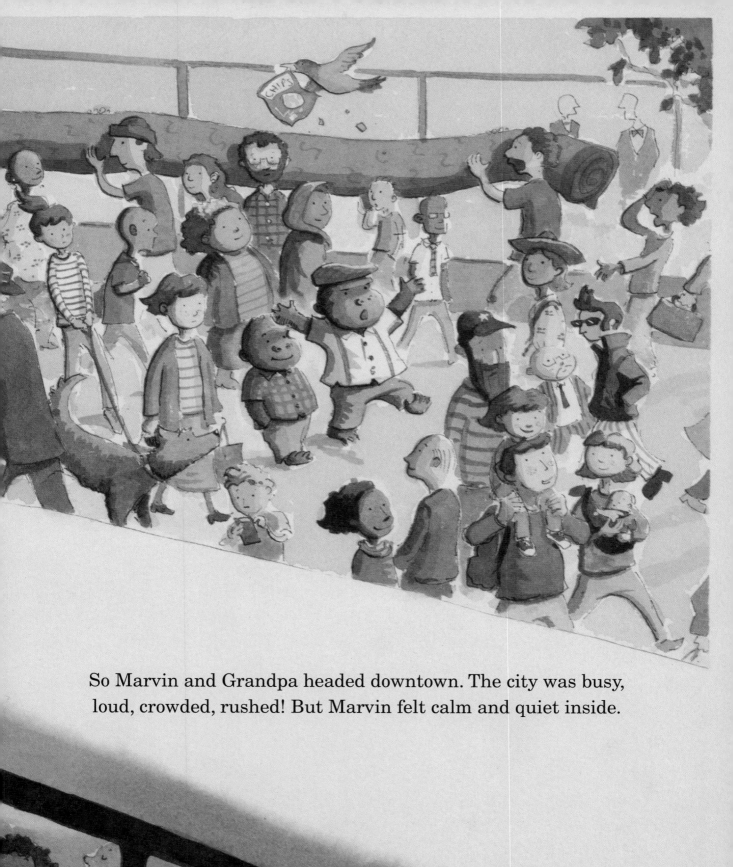

So Marvin and Grandpa headed downtown. The city was busy, loud, crowded, rushed! But Marvin felt calm and quiet inside.

On Monday, they ate bananas. Grandpa gobbled, but Marvin ate slowly, noticing the bright yellow outside and the sweet ripe inside.

"Gorillas never get anywhere staring at bananas all day," said Grandpa. "Let's go."

"But did you really taste it?"

"Of course I tasted it! I ate it, didn't I?"

Marvin smiled.

On Tuesday, they rode a ferry.

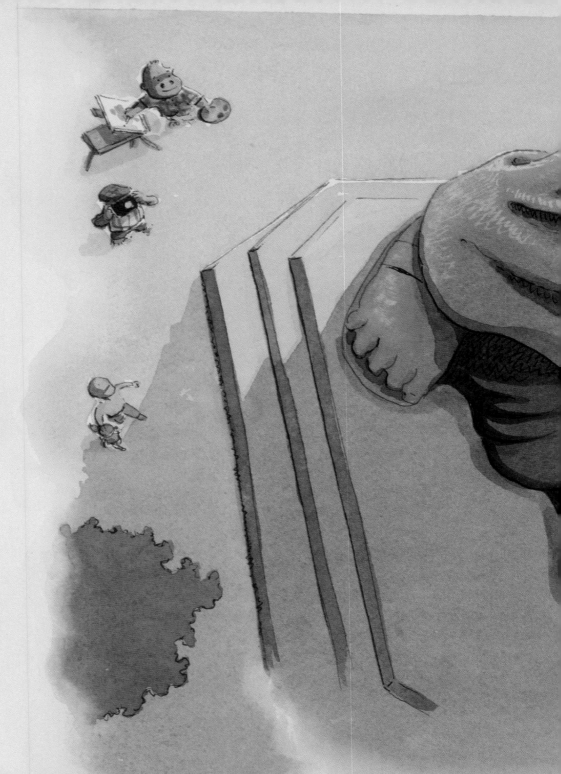

Grandpa took his camera, but Marvin took his time,
noticing shadows, curves, and colors.

Click. "I've seen it," said Grandpa. "Let's go."

"But did you really see it?"

"Of course I saw it! I looked at it, didn't I?"

Marvin smiled.

On Wednesday, they discovered a fountain.

"I wonder if the water is warm," said Marvin,
noticing drips and drops on his fingers.

Splash. "It's cold," said Grandpa. "Let's go."

"But did you really feel it?"

"Of course I felt it! I'm wet, aren't I?"

Marvin smiled.

On Thursday, they waited for a treat.

"It smells marvelous," said Marvin,
noticing the fragrant frosting and freshness.

"Yeah, yeah. Let's go," said Grandpa.

"But did you really smell it?"

"Of course I smelled it! I've got a nose, don't I? But this line
is too long! I want to thump thump roar right here!"

"Oh dear," said Marvin.

On Friday, they went to the symphony.

Marvin sighed as he listened,
noticing the notes swell and swirl.

"Do you really hear it, Grandpa?"

"Zzzzzzzz."

On Saturday, they arrived
at a tall building.

"Finally! We're going to
climb something and
pound our chests with a
thump thump roar!"

"Actually," said Marvin, "let's take the elevator."
So they swooshed to the top.
And when the doors opened…

Grandpa paused. He looked. He listened.
He smelled. He noticed everything around him.
And the thump thump roar inside him
felt smaller and smaller.

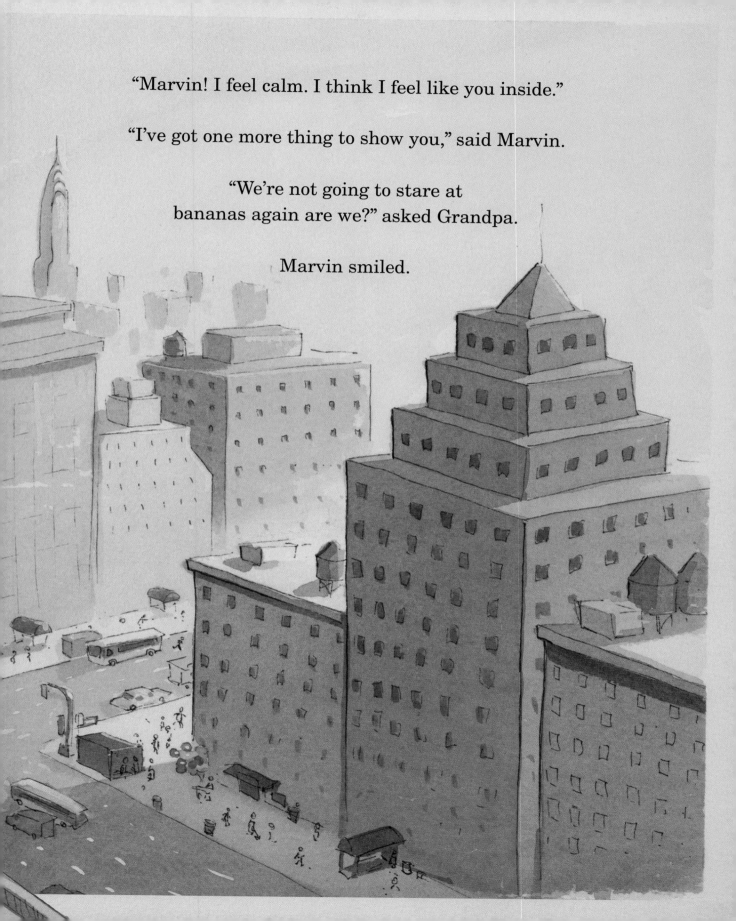

"Marvin! I feel calm. I think I feel like you inside."

"I've got one more thing to show you," said Marvin.

"We're not going to stare at
bananas again are we?" asked Grandpa.

Marvin smiled.

On Sunday, they visited a museum and
a whole bunch of people were staring at a banana!

Grandpa looked, too, and he *really* looked this time.

Grandpa smiled.

"King Calm," said Grandpa, "you're okay.
Come on, King. I'll buy you a banana."

READER'S NOTE

Have you ever sat in a movie theater with a bag of popcorn on your lap, and when you looked down, somehow the popcorn had disappeared? Or have you set your keys down somewhere, and then had no idea where you put them?

It happens to all of us, and these are great examples of how, sometimes, we are "mindless" in our actions. We're paying attention—we're just not thinking about what it is we're paying attention to! Just like Marvin's grandfather, we get distracted by life—often rushing through it. And when that happens, we miss some pretty amazing stuff.

We can't take all the blame for not paying attention to everything around us. Our brains are built to focus on some details, while skipping the rest. When we are busy or overwhelmed, our brains zone in on what is absolutely necessary to get tasks done efficiently, while letting the routine stuff run on autopilot. But here's the challenge: we tend to be busy and overwhelmed A LOT these days! Sometimes leaving so much on autopilot can mean we're not truly present in our lives for huge chunks of the day. Add to that our worry about what happened yesterday, or what's coming tomorrow, and we can miss enjoying today.

So how can we become more fully aware of what is happening around us—which, in turn, allows us to feel more fully alive? How can we be more like Marvin? And how can we help our kids be more like Marvin, too?

WHAT IS MINDFULNESS?

Mindfulness is one strategy that can help. We've probably all heard the word "mindful," but when we are talking about mindfulness as an approach to life, we are talking about something different. We are talking about very purposefully paying attention to what is going on in the present moment, without worrying about the past or the future, and without judging ourselves in the present. When we are mindful we focus on our thoughts, feelings, and what is going on in our bodies—and accept whatever that might be. We slow down, and notice the world around us. We also become aware of things we had no idea we were missing!

You may have heard of mindfulness in relation to Eastern philosophies, and that's where it started. But mindfulness has moved well beyond any one religion. Mindfulness has gone mainstream. It is practiced by people from all walks of life, and from many systems of belief. Anyone, including children, can benefit from becoming more mindful.

Mindfulness may sound a bit strange if you haven't tried it before, but there is lots of evidence that it works. In fact, it works so well that it's been used in psychology, healthcare, neuroscience, business, the military, education, and beyond! Mindfulness has been shown to be good for our bodies, minds, mood, and stress levels. It can help us get along better with others. It can also improve our self-awareness and help us manage our thoughts and behaviors. Being mindful can help us slow down and make decisions reflectively rather than reflexively. Mindfulness can even lead to positive changes in our brains that are linked to learning and memory. And, perhaps most importantly, it can help us feel calm, peaceful, hopeful, and happy. No wonder it supports academic and life success! Marvin had the right idea all along.

So how can you and your child practice focusing your attention and becoming more mindful? Well, how do we generally attend to the world around us? Through our senses, of course! Our senses are a great way to become more aware of ourselves and our surroundings. Unfortunately, most of what they tell us barely registers in our awareness. But just like Marvin, by noticing—really noticing—what our senses are revealing, we can keep some wonderful things from slipping by. Try tuning in to your senses in a very intentional way. Here are some strategies to heighten your awareness as you take a mindful tour through the senses.

Mindful Tasting: Mindful tasting involves noticing what you are eating, rather than just popping food in your mouth and gobbling it down so you can move on to something else. The next time you share a meal or snack with your child, slow down and follow these steps together. Hold the food in your mouth for a few seconds before you begin to chew. Then taste without biting. Finally, chew slowly before you swallow. Savor the food. Notice its flavor, texture, and temperature. How would you describe it? Use lots of different words—crunchy, smooth, creamy, bitter—as you really taste it. Try this strategy with foods you like, and with foods you don't like, too. Imagine how different foods taste. Which ones are similar? Which ones are different? Try variations of the same food, for example, by sampling three kinds of apples. Make sure to involve all your other senses, too. Consider the appearance, feel, and smell of the food. Listen to it sizzle as it cooks, or the sound it makes as you take a bite. Food can be a wonderful part of the day if you truly experience it, so take it off autopilot. Think of Marvin and take your time!

Mindful Seeing: You can practice mindful seeing by simply stopping and describing what is around you. When you are at the park with your child, ask what your child sees. Or try looking for objects of a specific size, shape, or color. Taking pictures can help you tune into details, too—as long as you're not a quick point-and-shoot photographer like Grandpa! Try painting what you see. Experiment with mixing colors until you create the perfect match for your child's t-shirt or a favorite stuffed animal. Watch a snow globe until the last snowflake settles. Use nature as your canvas; find shapes in the clouds or watch raindrops slide down a window and gather speed as they merge together. Follow an ant around your backyard. There are also many fun books that focus on careful looking, like *I Spy* or *Where's Waldo?*

Mindful Feeling: The next time you sit down with your child, try noticing how the chairs feel. Are they comfortable? Are they hard or soft? Does the back rest against you, or push against your spine? Or try mentally scanning your bodies from head to toe, noticing anything you feel. Are your clothes comfortable? Are

your shoes too tight? Play games involving touch. Hide various items in a paper bag and have your child guess the hidden objects just by feeling them. Go on a treasure hunt through the house searching for items that are soft, hard, smooth, rough, fuzzy, or bumpy. A bath or shower can also provide opportunities for mindfulness. Is the water hot or cold? How does the soap feel? Is the towel nice and soft?

Mindful Smelling: Discuss smells you like and don't like with your child. How would you describe them? Bake a treat together and notice the aroma wafting through the house. Then go outside. Come back in and experience the wonderful aroma all over again. Open the fridge and smell what you find. Plays games with smell. Have your child close his or her eyes and smell vinegar, vanilla, coffee, or cocoa. Can your child identify them? Which scent is your child's favorite? Have fun with scratch and sniff stickers!

Mindful Listening: Close your eyes with your child and listen to the sounds around you. What do you notice? Close your eyes again. Is there anything you missed the first time? Choose sounds to focus on. Listen to music and try to pick out different elements, like the vocals or drums. Play a sound that resonates, like a note on a piano, triangle, or bell, and listen until the sound is completely gone. Try sound matching, too. Find something that makes a particular sound, like a piggybank, and hunt through the house until you find something that sounds similar, like a jar of buttons.

Mindfully experiencing the world through all of your senses is a great way for you and your child to become calmer, more focused, and more tuned in—just like Marvin! So turn off the autopilot and really start tasting, seeing, feeling, smelling, and listening to the Great Big World around you!

ABOUT THE AUTHORS

Susan D. Sweet, PhD, is a clinical child psychologist and mother of two. She has worked in hospital, school, and community-based settings and is passionate about children's mental health and well-being. She is the co-author of *Princess Penelopea Hates Peas: A Tale of Picky Eating and Avoiding Catastropeas* and *Cinderstella: A Tale of Planets Not Princes*. Susan strives to be mindful, but still misses a moment or two. None of them involve chocolate.

Brenda S. Miles, PhD, is a pediatric neuropsychologist who has worked in hospital, rehabilitation, and school settings. She loves cool jazz, warm waves, puffy clouds, purple lilacs, and the taste of slightly green bananas. She is an author and co-author of several books for children, including *Imagine a Rainbow: A Child's Guide for Soothing Pain* and *Move Your Mood!* This is her first book about gorillas.

ABOUT THE ILLUSTRATOR

Bryan Langdo is the illustrator of over 30 books for children and the author of two. His picture book *Tornado Slim & the Magic Cowboy Hat* (Two Lions, 2012) won a 2013 Spur Award for Storytelling from Western Writers of America. Bryan lives in Hopewell, New Jersey, with his wife and two children. When he's not working, he likes to be in the woods.

ABOUT MAGINATION PRESS

Magination Press is an imprint of the American Psychological Association, the largest scientific and professional organization representing psychologists in the United States and the largest association of psychologists worldwide.